Tell me the Truth, Tom!

Also in the Totally Tom series:

2: Watch Out, Wayne
3: Get Lost, Lola
4: Keep the Noise Down, Kingsley
5: Drop Dead, Danielle!
6: Don't Make Me Laugh, Liam

Tell me the Truth, Tom!

Jenny Oldfield

Illustrated by
Neal Layton

a division of Hodder Headline Limited

First published in Great Britain in 2002
by Hodder Children's Books

10 9 8 7 6 5 4 3 2 1

A Catalogue record for this book is available
from the British Library

ISBN 0 340 85102 3

Printed and bound in Great Britain

Hodder Children's Books
A Division of Hodder Headline Ltd
338 Euston Road
London NW1 3BH

One

'Gerrup, Tom!'

Tom Bean lay on the ground holding his leg. He groaned and rolled over in the mud.

Mr Wright blew his silver whistle. The game stopped.

'Sir, he's fakin' it!' the Reds yelled, eager for play to go on.

'Oh-uh-ah!' Tom sighed. He clutched his knee as if in agony while the teacher jogged over to him.

'See, sir, there's nothing wrong with 'im!' Jack Farthing darted forward to grab Tom's arm and pull him to his feet.

'Er-erghhh!'

'Stand back, Jack!' Mr Wright ordered with a worried look.

'Sir, Jack tackled with both feet!' the Blue team cried. 'He went in from behind, he used his elbows!'

Through half-closed eyes, Tom saw the referee draw a red card from his tracksuit pocket and order Big Jack off the school soccer pitch.

'Three strikes and you're off!' the ref told Big Jack sternly.

Jack huffed and puffed, blowing clouds of steam into the cold, misty air. He muttered under his breath, then spread both arms wide. 'Sir, I didn't do nothink! I never even touched him!'

Tom thought he'd better do some more groaning.

'Ughh-uh-ergh!'

'Walk!' the ref ordered Jack. 'Now!'

Tom watched Jack hang his head and struggle, left-right, left-right through the fog to the touchline, like a whale wading through mud. Hiding a grin, he rolled on to all fours, then staggered to his feet.

'Are you OK?' Mr Wright checked.

Tom grunted and nodded. He hopped in a circle, going 'Ouch-ooch-ouch!'.

Little Jimmy Black ran by with the ball. 'Nice one, Heinz!' he whispered to Tom.

'Cool!' Kingsley Harris slapped Tom's shoulder. Without Big Jack, the Reds were down to ten men. As captain of the Blues, Kingsley took the ball from skinny Jimmy and got ready to take the free kick.

The ball was just outside the Reds' penalty area, there was a good chance of sneaking a last-minute goal. So Tom stopped ouching and sprinted into position. Now it didn't matter about being injured – the free kick had been given and that was that.

'Huh, look at 'im; it's a flipping miracle!' Jack yelled from the side of the pitch.

Kingsley aimed, kicked with his cannonball right foot and curved the ball over the wall of Reds, past the goalie and straight into the net.

'Goal!' Jimmy, Tom and the rest of the Blues leaped into the air, grabbed Kingsley and clambered over him. The whole lot of them went down in a cheering, slapping, muddy heap.

'2–1!' Mr Wright told them. Then he checked his watch and blew the final whistle.

'Cheat!' The Red team wasn't happy. 'Look what you did, sir! You gave 'em the game! 'S not fair!'

Too late! Tom got up out of the mud and did a little dance.

'2–1! 2–1!' he chanted. It was dead easy to fool Leftie Wright; he knew this because he did it at least three times a day! Wow, and wasn't it a great feeling when your team won! And who cared if you had mud in your hair, your mouth and down the back of your shorts? 2–1 was what it was all about.

Tom threw his arm around Kingsley's shoulder. They laughed and fooled around:

'What d'you get when you take the "h" out of Jack Farthing's second name?' Kingsley asked.

'Dunno. What do you get when you take the "h" out of Jack Farthing's second name?'

'A big stink!'

Kingsley's punchline sent Tom reeling off to the left, holding on to his stomach. He laughed so much he nearly choked.

Big Jack scowled as he lumbered by.

'Don't worry; even if he heard, he wouldn't get it!' Kingsley grinned. 'He's got a brain the size of a frozen pea!'

'2–1, 2–1!' Tom Heinz-Beanie-Bean sang out. And it was Thursday–burger, beans and chips for tea, with fresh doughnuts from Tesco if he was lucky. He sprinted across the playground, almost tripping full length over Fat Lennox, the caretaker's dog, asleep in the doorway.

'Grrrufff!' Lennox grumped.

'Gerrup out of the way, you stoopid dog!'

Tom swerved and ran on. He dodged into the boys' cloakroom, stuffed his uniform into his bag, then grabbed his skateboard.

'See ya, Heinz!' Jimmy called.

'Yeah, see ya!' Tom threw down his board and hopped on.

With a wave and a grin, he ollied over Lennox, down three steps. He kick-flipped and flicked his way back across the playground, then clunked, whirred, tilted and bunny-hopped all the way home.

'And it's the UK's Tom Bean landing a backside bluntslide and a frontside tailslide to fakie on the monster rail to take the win...!'

Tom didn't have a clue what it meant, but he'd read it in *Crusha* magazine and remembered it word for word. And it sounded good!

Neeeyaaah! He screeched around the corner into Hammett Street and tic-tacked down the cracked pavement,

bump-bump-bump.

'...And Heinz flips out with those flaming feet. He sticks a backside alley-oop tailslide and a nosegrind shove-it into his front garden...!'

'Watch it!' an old geezer walking his dog yelled at Tom. The dog went wild, snapping and barking, baring its teeth at Tom's board. Tom shot up the garden path and bailed at the front step. Shoving the door with his shoulder, he lunged inside the house.

'Mum, what's for tea? I'm starvin'!' Tom flung down his board and dumped his bag.

'So what's new?' Beth Bean replied from the kitchen. 'And it's beans, chips and burgers, as if you didn't know!'

'And doughnuts?' Tom demanded, charging down the hall.

'Where's the bag? Can I have one now?'

'Thomas Bean, what're you like! Take those boots off now!' His mum shook her head at the muddy mess that was her son.

The moment his boots were off, she shoved him upstairs.

'Don't touch the walls, make straight for the bathroom and get in that shower!'

'Uuh-ergh!' Tom hung back on the landing. Oh no, not the shower!

'What have you been doing, mud-wrestling?' Beth herded him into the bathroom and guarded the door.

'Blame Jack Stinky Farthing!' Tom protested. 'He fouled me outside the penalty box, then kicked mud all over me, then dragged me along the ground! Look, I'm limping!'

'Nice try, Tom, but you don't fool me! Come on, clothes off!'

'Aw, Mum!'

'Top, please!' Beth held out her hand while Tom struggled out of his football shirt.

'Socks!'

'I'm starvin'! Can't I have tea first?' Tom's socks were stiff with dried mud and grass

as he pulled them off.

'Shorts!' Beth insisted.

Tom pulled a face, but did as he was told, then shivered. 'Mum, it's freezin'!'

'Pants!' She turned on the shower and tucked the curtain inside the bath.

'No way!' He wasn't taking those off, not while she was in the room!

'Jump in like that then, and then hand me those muddy knickers from behind the curtain. Go on!'

'Ergh-huh-yuck!' The shower pricked his skin with hot, hissing drops. He huddled behind the curtain and handed over the soggy underpants. 'I bet this never happens to Robbie Exley after a match!'

'Yes, but you're not the star striker for Steelers, worth a million quid a year,' his mum pointed out. 'You're Tom Bean, aged 9–'

'–And a half!' he cut in.

'–The youngest of my four boys, and by far the most trouble!' Beth sighed. 'Always

up to something, playing tricks, or falling off that blessed board!'

'Why did you and Dad have me, then?' Tom had grabbed the shower gel and squirted giant blobs onto the sponge, squidging it until it came up in a mass of bubbles. He was planning a foam beard, to make him look like Father Christmas.

'Hey you, less of your cheek!' His mum backed away with her armful of muddy kit. 'And use shampoo on your hair, get yourself properly clean!'

'Yeah-yeah!' Tom wagged his head from side to side, dabbing foam onto his chin, then all over his chest.

'Oh, and by the way, did you win your match?' Beth called over her shoulder.

'Yeah, 4–1!' he crowed. Counting the offside goal and the one that hit the post!

Tom put his face under the shower and washed off his beard. They were a good team; him, Kingsley, Jimmy and the rest. Tomorrow, after school, he would get

Kingsley to teach him to do a shove-it. Yeah, good thinking! A new day, a new skateboarding trick. Live to skate! Yo dude, yeah!

Two

After his shower, Tom looked out of the window and saw that the light was on in the shed.

He went down, across the cold, damp yard and into the snug warmth of his dad's aviary.

Chirp-chirp, cheep-cheep, coo-coo! Twenty soft budgie-voices greeted him. A blue bird called Chippie fluttered from its perch onto

Tom's shoulder and did a little dance.

'Close the door, Tom.' Harry Bean emerged from a tiny back room where he kept the birdseed. At six foot three, he had to stoop low and squeeze himself through the narrow door. More birds left their perches and flew to peck seed from Harry's cupped hand. 'Did you win your match?' he asked.

'Yeah, 5-1!' Counting the offside, the one that hit the post AND the penalty that Jimmy missed.

'Did you score?'

'No, but I laid three on!' Well, he did, sort of. And it wasn't his fault that the strikers had failed to put the ball into the net!

'Good lad.' Tom's dad poured fresh water into the feeding dishes.

Tom took Chippie to drink. The tiny bird hopped down his arm and plop into the water, where he spread his wings and took a messy bath.

'Watch it!' Tom complained. Three tiny

drops of water had showered onto his cheek.

Chippie hopped out onto his hand and shook his feathers.

'Chip-chip-chippety-chip!' he squawked. 'Who's a cheeky boy? Chippety-chippety-chippety-chip!'

Tom pursed his lips and made a kissing sound. 'Where's Thomas?'

'Where's Thomas?' the budgie echoed. 'Chip-chippety-chip!'

Tom grinned then changed the subject. 'Da-ad, I've been thinkin'.'

'Uh-oh!'

'No, I have! I've decided what I want for Christmas.'

Big silence, except for the fluttering and pecking of budgies at their seed.

'Can you guess?'

'Yamaha motorbike?' Harry kidded.

'I'm serious, dad. I wanna pro board with a plain deck, riser pads, grip tape and mega fancy graphics!'

'Do you, now?' Harry didn't understand a word of skateboarding jargon. In his day, it had been plain old roller-skates, or nothing. 'Leave it with me. I'll have a word with your mum.'

Tom sighed and gazed around. Green, yellow and blue birds swung on swings, perched on perches and fluttered about. A special heat-lamp glowed from the sloping ceiling. 'Yeah,' he said dreamily. A cool set up, with Kingsley heading up the crew, skating through the centre of town, pulling wheelies and practising grinds–the coolest thing on the streets!

'Tom, do your work!'

'Tom Bean, are you listening to me?'

'Pay attention, Tom!'

'Tom, you really are the limit!'

Moan-moan-moan; that was all Tom ever got from the teachers.

Except for Leftie Wright. Leftie was OK. He sat on the edge of his desk and told jokes. He was a big Steelers fan. Tom had once lurked outside the staff-room door and overheard this:

Miss Ambler: *I hear Thomas Bean is in trouble with the Head again.*
Mrs Holmes: *Apparently, he was caught sticking chewing-gum on Danielle Hazelwood's chair.*

Miss Ambler: *Poor Danielle! I wouldn't trust that boy as far as I could throw him!*

Leftie: *I disagree. He's not a bad kid really.*

Mrs Holmes: *Not bad! I suppose you call crashing all the computers in the entire school 'not bad'! Or skateboarding indoors, or flooding the boys' toilets, or...!*

Leftie: *(chuckling) Oh, that stuff's just what you'd expect from him. He doesn't mean any harm. It's totally Tom!*

'What's up, Tom?' Mr Wright asked at the end of the day.

'Nothing.' Tom flung some homework books into his bag and barged towards the door, knocking into Danielle Hazelwood as he went.

'Ouch!' Danielle made a big deal out of it. 'Stop pushing, Tom!'

'Stop pushing, Tom!' he mimicked behind her back.

Leftie collared him for that. 'I don't want to see you being rude to other kids, you hear?'

'Yes sir.' The classroom was empty now. Tom was dying to get outside and join Kingsley.

'So what's up, tell me. Why are you in a bad mood?'

Tom decided to confess. 'Mum won't buy me a new board for Christmas.' She'd said they couldn't afford it. His manky old one with the missing wheel nut and chipped baseplate would have to do.

'And?' Leftie prompted.

'And school's boring, sir.'

'You mean, for an action man like you, sitting at your desk all day isn't much fun?'

'No sir. I mean, yes sir!' Tom fidgeted from foot to foot. At this rate, Kingsley would've gone off without him.

Leftie nodded. 'You're not wrong there, Tom. But just remember, school is something we all have to go through, like it

or not. And if we're clever, we do it without getting up teachers' noses or annoying other kids.'

Tom sighed. He felt a long lecture coming on.

'OK, OK!' Suddenly Leftie grinned. 'Get out of here before I make you tidy up my desk as punishment for banging into Danielle!'

So Tom shot off, picked up his skateboard and cap from the cloakroom and sprinted past Bernie King with his mop and bucket.

Hey, Heinz! Jimmy dribbled a ball across the wet playground. 2–1. Come on, you Blues!

'You seen Kingsley?" Jimmy asked him.

'I'm over here!' Tom's hero called. Kingsley was grinding down the long metal rail that ran down the side of the wide stone steps leading from the car park to the main playground. The grating sound of the trucks scraping the length of the pole brought Fat Lennox wheezing and growling

out of the main entrance.

Tom jumped on his own board and skated across. 'Hey, goofy!' he grinned at Kingsley, whose casual, left-footed style he admired.

Kingsley bailed by the steps to Bernie King's basement. 'You still wanna learn a shove-it?'

Nodding eagerly, Tom glanced around the dark playground. A few teachers' cars were

left in the car park, but there was plenty of space to learn a radical move.

'I'll show you.' Kingsley hopped back on board, jumped and flicked his deck around to face 180 degrees the other way. 'It's a back foot trick,' he explained. 'Try it.'

Tom tried. He leaned too hard on his back foot, crashed the tail against the tarmac and fell off.

Whack! His bum hit the ground.

'Press down with your front foot first.'

Second try. This time, Tom smacked the nose of the board down way too far and he tipped off face first. 'Hmm.' How come Kingsley made it look so easy?

'You gotta practise!' Already bored with Tom's clumsy efforts, Kingsley sprinted up the steps and did another brilliant grind.

'Grrrufff!' Lennox bared his teeth and dribbled.

Now Tom's mind was set on showing off too. Kingsley wasn't the only one who could do fancy moves. 'Watch me, I'm gonna ollie!'

Six steps were a lot to jump down–he'd only ever done four before. But he felt sure he could make it. So he set off downhill, gathering speed as an angry Lennox trundled alongside.

'Grrrrruffffff!' the fat bulldog snarled.

'Gerroff!' Tom yelled, wobbling as he reached the steps.

Then he was in the air, sailing, wobbling a bit more, landing clear of the steps but seriously off-balance. 'Woah-oh-oh!'

Another crash. Another bruise on his bum.

Tom stopped, but his board didn't. It went rolling and rattling on, straight towards Bernie's basement, with Lennox snapping at it.

'Grab it!' Kingsley warned.

Too late. Tom got up and scuttled after his board, but stupid Lennox got in the way. Before he could stop it, his precious deck had disappeared.

Bump-bump-bump! It rattled into the basement. Crash! It hit the tiny window next to Bernie's door. Tinkle-tinkle! The glass shattered and dropped. Tom's jaw fell and he stood fixed to the spot.

'What the...!' Bernie King thundered out of the main entrance and across the car park. He arrived panting and snarling.

'Don't tell me...Let me guess! Yep, a

skateboard straight through the window!'

Tom looked round to find that Kingsley had scarpered, the jammy thing.

Stomping down into his basement, the caretaker seized Tom's board. 'Tom Bean, in your time at Rowbridge Junior, you've broken just about every rule in the book, but this one takes the biscuit!'

It wasn't me! It was Jack Farthing!

Ooch-ouch, I've broken my leg! The excuses flashed through Tom's head, but he didn't get a chance to use any of them.

'NO SKATEBOARDING IN THE PLAYGROUND!' Bernie roared.

'Grrrrufff!' Lennox backed him up.

'It's a RULE! But no, you have to ignore it, and smash goes my window!' Bernie's eyes bulged. His face went red, his muscles almost burst through his brown overalls.

Tom gulped and backed away.

'WELL, THAT'S IT, I'VE HAD ENOUGH!' 'GRUFFFF!' *Me too!* Lennox waddled towards Tom and head-butted him.

'I INTEND TO INFORM THE HEAD!' Bernie just about had a heart attack. He shook the skateboard at Tom.
'AND I'M CONFISCATING THIS, YOU HEAR? YOU'RE GONNA GET IT BACK OVER MY DEAD BODY!'

Three

'The thing is, Chip, nobody cares!' Tom stood in the garden shed and complained to the blue budgie. 'Bernie's the King of Rowbridge Junior. They all do what he says, even Mrs Waymann. So when he stomps off and tells her about the broken window, she nods and says yeah, 'course Bernie can confiscate my board and what's more, she'll have a little word with me personally

tomorrow morning!'

Chippie chirped and flew onto Tom's shoulder. He sidled close to his cheek and nibbled his ear. *I hear what you're sayin', dude. Bummer, huh?*

'Talking of bums–I can't even sit down!' Tom moaned. 'I've got a MASSIVE bruise right here! But no one cares about that either!'

'Chippety-chip!' the bird said. *I know what you mean. It's tough.*

Tom knew he could tell Chippie everything, here in the warm silence of the shed. 'And now I've got no board, and Mum and Dad won't buy me a new one for Crimbo, and I can't practise shove-its, and the other kids will go off with Kingsley and forget about me!'

SHOCK NEWS: Tom Bean has quit the surfing scene after a short but promising career. His best trick was to ollie down twenty steps on to a big, gnarly ledge, taking some Superman chest slams on the way. Last seen doing a no-comply to tail on a bank to block, his board got stuck between a bank and a rail, flexed and bailed him. End of story. Sorry to hear it, Tom!

'So what do I do now, Chip?'

'Where's Thomas? Who's a cheeky boy?' the bird croaked. *Like, cheer up, dude. It's not the end of the world!*

'OK, so my board was pretty manky. There was that missing wheel nut and the deck was beginning to split, but it was all I had!'

The board had shared loads of crashes and slams with Tom. Every little scratch had a story behind it. Like the time Tom was connecting up a heel-flip with an ollie and smashed into a lamp-post. Or when he nailed a nollie in the park but didn't see the bench in front of him. Smack!

In fact, now Tom came to think about it, he liked that old board one heck of a lot!

'It's mine!' he grunted, while Chippie hopped on to his head. 'Bernie King can't just take it and stash it away in his office. It's not fair!'

Hey, dude, who said life was fair? Chippie leaned forward and pecked at Tom's eyebrow.

'But it isn't! Bernie's only the caretaker. He doesn't own the school!'

'Talking to yourself again, Beanie?' Tom's older brother, Nick, tapped on the window. 'They can lock you up for that, you know!'

'Get lost, Nick!'

Out in the yard, his big brother unchained his bike and cycled off in the dark to see his girlfriend, Zoe.

Tom frowned as he got Chippie to hop on his finger so he could pop him back on his perch. 'I gotta get my board back!' he muttered. 'I don't care what anyone says!'

'Thomas Bean, this time you've gone too far!' Mrs Waymann sat behind her giant desk and glared at her least favourite pupil. Tom shuffled on the worn rug. Wicked Witch Waymann was the Head's nickname. She had beady eyes and a bump on her nose. Her fingernails were long and red.

'I'm used to your practical jokes, young man. The time you snuck out of your PE lesson, into the changing room and hid everybody's school ties, for example. Or the occasion in assembly, when you pulled the plug to the music system out of its socket and left us high and dry in the middle of our song.'

Tom tried to hide a smile at the memory. Waymann had warbled on without realising, long after everyone else had stopped singing.

'It's not funny!' the Head snapped.

'No, Miss!'

'Don't call me Miss!'

'Sorry, Miss–er Mrs Waymann!'

'That's better. Now Thomas, you understand that what you did yesterday evening has landed you in by far the worst trouble yet!'

No kidding! Tom hadn't stopped thinking about his skateboard since it had gone whizzing through the basement window.

'It calls for severe punishment,' Waymann warned. 'First of all, I'm going to make you pay for the damage to the window.

I shall write to your parents suggesting

that they withhold your pocket money until the debt is paid. Secondly, I forbid you to play in the school football team for the rest of this season.'

Ouch! Tom felt that. No more soccer! Six months of standing on the touchline without being able to touch the ball! And him the team's star goal scorer (along with Kingsley and Jimmy).

'Third, I'm telling you loud and clear that your skateboard, which should never have been in school in the first place, will remain locked away in Mr King's basement until such time as I see fit to return it!' Waymann's glare grew sterner than ever.

Tom swallowed hard. Ouch, ouch, double-ouch! 'S not fair!

There was a long silence inside the big, perfumed room, broken by a sudden knock at the door.

'Come!' Waymann boomed.

The door opened and Lola Kidman from Tom's own class tiptoed in. 'Please Mrs

Waymann, Mr Wright says Tom Bean has to go straight to the school bus to join the swimming group after you've finished with him here.' Lola delivered the message in a silly, sing-song voice. She snuck a look at Tom–a look that said, 'Rather you than me!'

'Yes. Thank you Lola, dear. But please tell Mr Wright that Tom is suspended from swimming lessons for the rest of this term.'

Lola Kidman was the school breaststroke champion. She swam like a fish and dived from the highest board. Tom's punishment sent her pale with shock as she backed through the door.

Click! Tom's heart sank. No skateboarding, no soccer, and now no swimming!

Waymann pressed a button on her telephone. 'You may go!' she told him. 'And if I hear one more word about you misbehaving, you'll be in serious trouble, young man!'

'What's she call this then?' Tom groaned to Kingsley. Losing your skateboard was serious with a capital 'S'.

'I'll ask my cousin, Leon, if you can borrow his,' Kingsley promised.

'Cool.'

'...When he gets back from his visit to his gran and grandpa in Jamaica,' Kingsley added with a quick grin.

Yeah, in a million years! Tom thought. Jamaica wasn't exactly round the corner, was it?

'Sorry about your board, Tom!' Lola Kidman flung her swimming towel down under her desk. Her long, dark hair dripped onto the floor. 'Waymann didn't half look mad!'

'She was,' Tom sighed.

'Cheer up, Tom, it's not the end of the world,' Mr Wright told him as he herded the whole class into the hall for wet dinner break.

'You can hang around with Lola and me,' Sasha Johnson invited.

Danielle giggled and whispered to her best mate, Bex. 'Sasha Johnson fancies Tom Bean!' Tom heard her say.

Ergh! He marched off in disgust to find an empty table.

'Come on, what's so bad?' Mr Wright strolled up to Tom, hands in his tracksuit pockets.

An idea flashed into Tom's mind. Maybe he could work on soft-hearted Leftie to get his board back for him. 'The thing is, sir, that skateboard doesn't even belong to me!'

'It doesn't? How come?'

'It's my cousin, Leon's. He let me borrow it while he's away visiting family!'

'That was nice of him.' The teacher fell for

thought it was safe to sneak away and scout around the entrance to Bernie King's room. But now moody, mardy Danielle and teacher's pet Bex had tracked him down.

'Don't even think about it, Tom!' Bex said in that soft, sensible way of hers. 'If you try to get your board back, you're gonna end up in even more trouble.'

'Who said anything about getting my board back?' Tom said huffily. 'Why don't you two go and poke your noses into someone else's stuff?'

He glared at Danielle, with her smooth, fair, girly-girl hair and at Bex in her neat and tidy shirt and tie.

'It's obvious that's what you're doing,' Danielle insisted. 'And believe me, Tom, it's not worth it!'

'Who asked you?' Turning his back, he studied the broken window. Bernie King had boarded it up to stop anyone climbing in. He would have to use a burglar-type lever to pull the board off again.

'You'll see!' Bex told him, walking off arm in arm with Danielle. 'And don't say we didn't warn you!'

'Nah-nah!' he breathed. But the girls had made him think twice.

OK, so it would look dead obvious if he just broke in and nicked the board. But no one could prove it if he didn't leave any clues. That meant no fingerprints, and a foolproof alibi.

This is getting a teenie weenie bit tricky! the small voice in his head pointed out.

'Grrrruffff!' Fat Lennox bounded up the basement steps and added to his problems.

Tom beat a retreat before Bernie King himself came out of his office, bashing into Jack Farthing who was leaning against the sports hall wall with a bunch of mates.

'Hey, watch it, Beanie!' Stinky yelled. He pushed Tom over, then laughed.

Tom picked himself up and hopped on one foot. He'd twisted his ankle for real this time. 'Watch it yourself!' he mumbled.

'Ah, did diddums hurt himself?' Jack jeered. 'Did he break his leg when he fell over?'

'Get lost!'

'Get lost yourself!' Jack acted the hard man in front of Ryan and Kalid.

'You gonna make me?'

Jack lunged at him and missed as Tom dodged and darted away.

'Yah, just like you, Tom Bean!' he cried. 'Chicken!'

'The bell's gone!' A girl's voice broke in. It was Lola, sprinting up the hill towards the main door. Her news broke up the group just at the point when things were getting nasty. Kalid and Ryan broke away, with Big Jack muttering and making chuck-chucking sounds over his shoulder.

Saved by the bell! Gingerly Tom took his weight on the injured ankle and trotted alongside Lola. Weird; it looked like no one else had heard the bell ring either.

'It didn't really!' she grinned. 'I just said

that to make Jack back off.'

Tom nodded. 'Good thinking!' Lola Kidman was OK.

'D'you want me to help you break into Bernie's office and get your board back?' she asked casually. Then she smiled at Tom and added, 'And yeah it IS that obvious, even to a pea brain like Jack!'

Lola was more than OK, she was a mate, Tom decided. She'd promised to give him the alibi he needed when he carried out the heist.

'I'll say you were at the swimming pool, watching me train,' she'd suggested. 'And I won't breathe a word about what you were really up to!'

'Lola Kidman

fancies Tom Bean!' Danielle had sniggered when she'd seen them whispering together in registration.

'Woo-wooh!'

Tom had ignored her. 'I'm off to the pool after school to watch Lola train,' he'd told his mum, on her way home from dinner duty.

'Well, as long as you keep out of trouble,' Beth had replied wearily. 'Tea's at half-five. Don't be late.'

And now it was four o'clock and Tom was lurking behind the sports hall, waiting for Leftie to blow his whistle and bring the soccer training session to a close.

'Foul! Ref, it's a free-kick! Referee!' The appeals

floated up from the soccer pitch to Tom's hiding place. He saw the last dim rays of daylight give way to the grey murk of a winter's evening, then heard Mr Wright blow the whistle to bring the teams off the pitch. This was it! In ten minutes, after the kids had changed out of their soccer strips, the school would be empty.

Tom waited a while longer. He heard Kingsley yell bye to Ryan, then saw the lights inside the building go off one by one. Last of all, he spotted Jack Farthing climbing into his dad's posh car and being swished away.

Right then, this was definitely it! Tom took a deep breath.

You know what happens if you get caught! the annoying little voice started up. *Waymann's given you your final warning. Next time she'll probably kick you out of Rowbridge for good.*

'I won't get caught!' Tom muttered through gritted teeth. 'There won't be a next time, will there.'

Says you!

'Not with this!' Tom dipped into his bag and drew out a steel ruler; the object he'd carefully chosen to help him commit his crime.

You've seen what happens on The Bill! The thief breaks in and sets off every alarm in sight. The cops arrive, sirens blaring – da-dah, da-dah, da-dah! They swarm in and make an arrest. Curtains for the villain. Life behind bars!

Tom's hand shook, but he began to creep across the dark playground towards the basement. His skateboard meant more to him than any of the scary stuff going on inside his head.

Da-dah, da-dah! In the distance a siren sounded, drew nearer, then faded away.

Waiting for his heartbeat to get back to normal, Tom went on. The basement steps looked dark and spooky, the big school building towered over him.

Wish I had a torch! he thought. Out on the street, the orange glare of street-lights and the dazzle of car headlamps made the empty school seem darker still. One step at a time, inch by inch he drew near the basement.

Stop! Think about what you're doing! the stupid voice began again.

Tom swallowed and gripped the ruler tight. All he had to do was lever the board off and crawl in through the broken window. His skateboard was almost within reach!

Thump-thump-thump! His heart acted up again, practically jumping out of his chest as he made his way down the basement steps. It was pitch black down here, and silent as a grave.

Thomas Bean, I sentence you to ten years in prison for breaking into Rowbridge Junior School! the Voice boomed.

Tom breathed out heavily and felt his way forward. He put his hand up to the place

where the wooden board should be, ready to jemmy it free.

Tom, how could you do this to us? It was his mum's voice, tearful and sobbing.

Oh, son! was all his heartbroken dad said.

'OK then, I won't!' he said, sitting down heavily on the bottom step. He wouldn't break in–end of story.

By this time, Tom's eyes were used to the darkness and he took one last sad look at the basement door and the small window beside it.

Huh? He blinked and looked again. How come?

The board was already off and the door stood open. It creaked on its hinges–eee-eak-eee!

Tom felt the hair at the back of his neck stand on end. Someone–another burglar–had beaten him to it! He might even still be in there, at this very moment putting his thieving hands on Tom's precious board.

Eeeakkk! The door swung gently open.

'Who's there?' Tom whispered.

There was no answer. So holding his ruler like a sword, he crept forward, ready to defend his skateboard to the death. Puh! He held his nose and stopped breathing. The stink in here was worse than anything he'd ever smelt. A sharp, hot animal stink that got up your nostrils and made your eyes water.

'Phwoah, Lennox!' Tom blamed the caretaker's dog and a severe case of bad breath. How on earth could Bernie put up with this? It was enough to make Tom back straight out.

But first, since fate had intervened, he had to rescue his board.

It was here somewhere–safely stowed away by Bernie. On his table, maybe, or up on a shelf on the back wall.

Tom fumbled his way around the office, stubbing his toe and bumping into furniture.

In the far corner, something stirred.

He froze. Animal or human–something was down here with him!

Desperately Tom tried to make out the shape that was moving in the corner. It seemed low to the ground on all fours, lean, with a long, bushy tail.

Animal, then. But not Lennox, whose barrel-shaped body and stumpy tail would have given him away.

Two yellow eyes glowed fiercely as the creature raised its head. There was a gleam of savage white teeth, and a snarl from the back of its throat.

Tom fixed his gaze on those fiery eyes. The stink overpowered him, and the stealth of the creeping, sharp-eared animal as it advanced out of its corner.

'Fox!' Tom gasped.

Up close, eyes flashing, teeth bared!
Fox! Sleek and fierce and stinking!
Opening its jaws and leaping towards Tom. Brushing against him as it shot by, disappearing faster than the eye could see, out of the basement door and up the steps into the open. Gone before Tom could even blink.

Five

'What's that pong?' Nick asked.

'What pong?' Harry Bean peered over the top of his evening newspaper and sniffed the air. 'Oh yeah, that pong.'

'It's you, Tom!' Nick came close and caught the whiff of fox.

'Pwoah, that stinks!'

'Gerroff!' Tom pushed his brother away.

'Shower for you, my lad!' his mum said as

she switched on the Six O'Clock News.

'I had one yesterday!' he cried feebly.

'Goodness knows how you picked up a smell like that from the swimming pool,' Beth commented. 'You're not telling me it's the chemical they put in the water!'

'More like fox-stink,' Know-all Nick said.

'Get lost!' Tom stamped off, up to the bathroom. The quicker he washed the smell away, the less likely he was to have to come up with an explanation.

Steeling himself to stand under the shower, he had time to look back on the whole fox-in-the-basement incident.

First and most important, he'd legged it without his board. How stupid was that? To let a stinky fox scare him half to death and make him run away without the thing he'd come for. Second, he'd dropped his steel ruler in the rush to get away.

And the ruler had his initials, T. C. B. (Thomas Callum Bean), scratched into its surface. Talk about careless!

He'd left the biggest clue for Bernie to find, and soon they'd be pinning the break-in onto him, and he wasn't even guilty!

So, who was? And how big a coincidence was it that someone else had decided to break into Bernie King's office at the exact same time as Tom?

No answers came to Tom in the clouds of steam.

And he hadn't got any further towards solving the mystery when he showed up, squeaky clean, at Hammett Street Youth Club that same evening.

'How did you get on?' Lola was the first to ask. She was dressed in tracksuit and trainers, fresh from the swimming pool.

'OK,' Tom lied.

'Did you get your board back?'

'Erm, no.'

'No!' Her squeaky surprise brought other kids drifting across.

'No, but I did see something else.' Tom had to cover up his failure, and fast. 'You'll

never guess what lives down there in Bernie King's basement!'

Kalid, Ryan, Kingsley, Lola and Sasha formed a circle around him. In the background, music blared and kids played snooker and table football.

'You're right, we'll never guess!' Kingsley prompted from under the peak of his baseball cap.

'Have a try.' Tom strung it out, taking attention off the fact that he was still skateboard-less. 'Go on, what lives in the basement?'

'Spiders,' Sasha suggested shyly.

'Rats,' Lola said with an eager look.

'A mad woman who thinks she's a witch!' Ryan chipped in.

'No, that's Waymann!' Kalid told him. 'She's got her own office.'

The gang fell about laughing.

'You're not even warm,' Tom told them. 'I'll have to tell you. It was a FOX!'

'You're joking!' Sasha breathed. 'A real live fox in Bernie's basement?'

'No kidding. His teeth were this big, and he had ginormous yellow eyes. He pounced on me and grabbed me by the throat. I had to fight him off with my bare hands!'

'Wow!' Ryan was impressed.

'Sure it wasn't a wolf, Heinz?' Kingsley kidded. 'A big, bad Red-Riding-Hood wolf that came creeping out of the forest to

eat us all up!'

Tom tutted. 'The fox had his teeth right here, like this! But I got hold of his jaw and opened his mouth. I forced him back and did a karate kick, hah-so!' He demonstrated a kick-boxing move, fast as lightning.

'Or a panther or a lion?' Kingsley wanted to know. 'Maybe even a man-eating tiger that vanished into the night!'

Kingsley was such a loudmouth when he wanted to be. Tom gave him a cold stare. 'I'm telling you, it was a F-O-X, fox!'

'Hey, there's a fox in the school basement!' Lola and Sasha spread the news. 'It attacked Tom Bean. It's really, really fierce!'

As word went round, Tom strutted his stuff. He was a fearless fighter, a superhero! There was no one else in this room who had ever fought a fox with his bare hands and won!

But then he began to hear a few comments like, 'No way!, and 'Dream on,

Tom!' from people like Danielle Hazelwood and Bex (Little Miss Sensible) Stevens.

'Don't listen to him,' Danielle told Sasha. 'You can never believe a thing Tom says!'

And Bex gave out the same message loud and clear. 'You know what he's like, always joking and making things up. It's what boys do!'

Yeah, the fox story is typical,' Danielle added. 'Before we know it, Bernie King will be keeping a whole zoo in his cellar. But you're not meant to believe it. It's just Tom telling stories with that wild imagination of his–totally Tom!'

'I'll show 'em!' Tom vowed.

He was walking home from the youth club with Ryan and his big sister, Sophie. Ryan was practising being an American air force pilot, swooping round lamp posts with his arms spread wide.

'Neeeyah–whoosh–vroom!' Ryan did a U-turn, banking his wings steeply. 'How will

you show 'em?' he asked Tom.

'I'll prove there's a fox in the basement!'

Sophie was talking into her mobile phone; on and on about how she would get her hair cut and what colour she wanted it.

Ryan whooshed and vroomed across her

path, then swerved back.

'How?' he said again.

'I'll take a camera and lie in wait for it to come back.' Tom made the plan on the spur of the moment, without thinking it through.

Whose camera? And wouldn't it be

asking for trouble to return to that damp, dark basement, where he'd already dropped his ruler with his initials on?

'I'll take a flash photograph,' he promised. 'Then people will have to believe me!'

'Neeyah!' Ryan said, rising to 20,000 feet and dive-bombing the pigeons outside St Martin's Church. 'Good thinking, Flight Lieutenant. 10-4, over and out!'

'Yeah, totally Tom!' Danielle jeered next morning, before registration. 'Not only does he fail to get his skateboard back, but he makes up some story about a fox!' She was the one who wouldn't let it drop, along with Stinky Farthing.

'What's this?' Jack strode up to Tom in the playground. He hadn't been around when the wild rumours flew at the youth club, and now he wanted to gloat big time. 'Poor little Tom; still no skatey-watey board, ah diddums!'

'Get lost, Jack!' Tom had enough

problems already. For a start, there was the ruler with his initials on, which someone was bound to find sooner or later. And second, big brother Nick had refused to lend him his camera.

'Pleee-eease!' Tom had begged at breakfast. 'I need it. It's important.'

'No way.' With two short words Nick had dashed Tom's hopes.

And his mum had set her seal on the situation with, 'Leave it, Tom. Zoe gave Nick that camera for his birthday. It's too good for you to be messing around with.'

No comment from his dad, who had dashed in for a quick coffee then out again to carry on delivering the mail.

'Thanks a million!' Tom had muttered bitterly. That camera was the only hope he had of convincing people that he was telling the truth about the fox!

And now he was in school, and it felt like a giant sword was hanging over his head. The

blade hovered, glinting in the sun, held only by a slim thread. When the thread broke, the sword would swoop and pierce him through the heart...

Jack Farthing followed him to the classroom, barging him with his elbow and tripping him up as they went.

'Thomas Bean, walk properly!' Mrs Holmes bellowed down the corridor.

'Can't even get his precious board back!' Jack crowed.

Tom stopped dead. 'What's your problem?' he demanded. 'What did I ever do to you?'

Jack pretended to be scared. 'Don't be mad, Tom. Look, I'm shaking all over!' He stuck out his arms and made them tremble.

'Hey, Jack, what happened to you?' Kalid demanded, pushing past them both into the classroom. He pointed at the heavy bandage around Jack's wrist.

'Nothing!' Jack brushed the question aside.

'Will you be fit for the match tomorrow?'

'Yeah, no problem. I said it was nothing, didn't I?'

Tom frowned, then grabbed the chance to follow Kalid into the room. But before he reached his seat on the back row, Jack caught up with him again. 'You're in dead trouble, Beanie-Baby, you know that don't you!'

'I said, lay off!' Tom muttered.

But Big Jack ignored him. 'They know it was you who broke in last night. You're for it, just you wait!'

'Well, if you must know, I didn't have to!, Tom sat down beside Kingsley. 'Bernie's door was open, so I just walked in!'

'Ha!' Jack laughed in his face. 'Like, yeah, we all believe that!'

'Uh-hum!' From the front desk Leftie coughed loudly. 'Jack and Tom, have you got something you'd like to share with us?'

'No sir, sorry sir!' Tom shook his head and turned red.

Jack stared coolly back, eyeball to eyeball with the teacher.

'Good. Then let's get on with this morning's notices, shall we?'

Mr Wright was halfway through announcing the soccer team for Saturday's match against Elton Juniors when the door burst open and Bernie King stormed in.

Uh-oh! Tom's heart jumped into his mouth.

What did I tell you? the small, smug voice inside his head started up again. *You just took one risk too many, and now you have to pay!*

Tom pictured what was to come–being dragged to Waymann's room, accused, sentenced without trial.

Bernie drew a deep breath to make his big announcement. 'No h-assembly this mornin'!'

Tom gulped. Had he heard that right? Bernie had forgotten something. Surely he was meant to say the long overdue words,

'Mrs Waymann wants to have a word with Thomas Bean in her room, right away!'

But no, he said it again. 'No h-assembly on account of the fact that there's an 'orrible stink in the 'all!'

'A horrible stink?' Leftie repeated.

'We think it's a problem with the drains,' Bernie informed him. 'On 'Ealth and Safety grounds, no one is allowed in the 'all

until further notice!'

'Great–no assembly! No music practice! No PE!' Whispers ran around the room.

Jack Farthing snuck a sly look at Tom's relieved face.

'You think you're off the hook!' he sneered. 'But don't you believe it!'

Six

'Count yourself lucky, babe!' Beth was fed up with Tom moping around the house. It was Saturday morning. Usually he would be scooting round looking for his footie kit, eager to get stuck into another needle match against one of the local junior schools.

But not today. Today Tom was banned from the team. And for every other Saturday until the end of the season.

So when his mum followed him into the aviary and called him lucky, he groaned and turned his back.

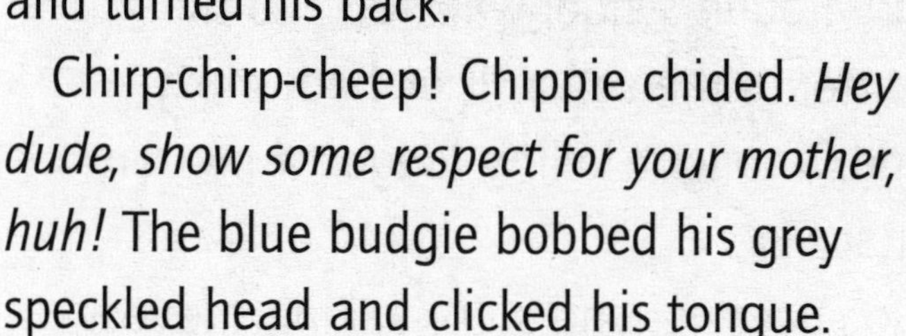

Chirp-chirp-cheep! Chippie chided. *Hey dude, show some respect for your mother, huh!* The blue budgie bobbed his grey speckled head and clicked his tongue.

'I mean it, Tom! You could've been in much worse trouble over this skateboard thing. It's only because Mrs Waymann's mind is on other things right now that you've got away so far with a good dressing down!'

He knew it was true, thinking back to yesterday, when men in overalls had crawled all over the building, trying to track down the mystery stink. 'If we can't pin it down by Monday, we'll have to close the whole school,' the Health and Safety people had warned the Head.

And three hundred kids had knelt down and prayed. While Tom had kept his thoughts to himself. To him, 'horrible stink' meant only one thing. Fox!

Never mind Bernie's drain theory. The pong around school was down to the squatter in the cellar. They had a foxy friend, a tongue-lolling lodger, a mystery menace...

'So cheer up, and stop making the rest of us feel miserable,' Beth went on.

Yeah, dude. You really pushed your envelope this time! Chippie added. 'Cheep-cheep-chippety-chip!' *You came unstuck good style. But hey, take it on the chin like a man!*

Tom frowned at the perky budgie. 'Whose side are you on?' Perching on Tom's shoulder, Chippie rolled his beady eye but said nothing.

'Tell you what, kid...' Harry Bean stooped low and came out of the food store at the back of the shed. A dozen budgies fluttered from their perches and disturbed the still air. Feathers flew and drifted to the floor.

'Why not get yourself along to watch the match this morning? Even if you can't play, I'm sure the team could do with your support.'

Huh; just like his dad to suggest being the nice guy!

'Yeah, I know.' Harry sucked his breath through clenched teeth. 'Tough, huh? But it'd mean a lot to Kingsley, Jimmy and the rest.'

Tom didn't know if he could bear to stand on the sideline and watch. Then again, it wouldn't do any harm to hang around when the school was almost empty...Fox! he thought. If only I could solve the mystery of the stink, I'd be in Waymann's good books again.

Yo, but three hundred kids would kill you! Chippie reminded him.

What for?

For robbing them of extra days off, dummy! If you snap the fox and prove he exists, they'll flush him out, and then

curtains for stinky-face. No more bad smells, so they won't have to close the school after all. End of story! Hmm. Big decision. Tom was stretched on the rack of doubt.

'Yes, get yourself down there!' his mum encouraged. She turned him around and marched him out, across the yard into the house, one-two, one-two! 'Here's your bus fare.'

'Hey, monkey face, you still want to borrow my digital camera?' Nick said in passing. 'Cos if you do, it's on top of my chest of drawers.'

Nick's gob-smacking personality transplant made up Tom's mind. He shot upstairs and seized the camera. Don't ask questions, get out of the house before Nick thinks twice!

Without pausing, he made a grab for his baseball cap and then his skateboard. Uh-oh, no board! 'Course not. But he was on a mission–sprinting to the bus stop, leaping on, then off outside the school as Elton's

team arrived for the match, checking the buttons on Nick's camera, zooming in on Bernie's basement, ready to capture that sly fox the second he dared to venture out!

He sought him here, he sought him there,
He sought that darned fox everywhere!

Out in the frosty playground, by the sports hall, in the spiky holly bushes by the main entrance, Tom scouted for the fox.

'Hey, Heinz!' Jimmy greeted him as he trotted out of the boys' changing room.

'Wish us luck!'

'You won't need it,' Tom assured him. 'You'll murder Elton, no problem!'

'Yeah, but I wish you were playing.'

'Me too,' Tom murmured, standing aside as the rest of the Rowbridge team followed Jimmy, all dressed in their smart blue and white kit. There was Kingsley and Kalid, Ryan and Big Jack Farthing, who saw Tom and couldn't resist a sneer.

Soon after, Elton Juniors appeared in yellow and green. They ran onto the pitch, heads up, chests out, under the eagle eye of their games teacher and referee for the day, Miss Rawlings.

For a few minutes, Tom stood at a distance and watched the two teams kick the ball around. But it hurt too much not to be out there with them, so he let his shoulders sag and turned away.

'Watch it, Tom Bean!' Bernie King warned from across the playground.

'What? I'm not doin' anythin'!' Tom

protested in a high, whiney voice.

'Exactly. Just watch it, that's all!' Bernie disappeared into the school with Fat Lennox at his heels.

'Hough-hough-hough!' went the wheezy dog. Waddle-waddle, cough-cough!

Wheeee! Miss Rawlings blew the whistle for the start of the match, while Leftie kept a cautious eye on his team from the touchline.

Better find that fox fast! Tom decided. Stealthily he crept down the side of the building, peering in through iced-up windows, sliding and skidding down slopes and slipping between tall walls, into dark corners where a fox might hide.

Sniff-sniff! Every step he took, Tom was smelling his way. He smelt the frozen flower beds and the tall pine trees that flanked the school entrance. He caught the pong of old school dinners from the drain outside Bernie King's office, and a whiff of chemicals from the science lab.

'I told you once already; beat it!' Bernie popped up again out of the blue.

Flash! The camera went off in Tom's nervous fingers, capturing a slanting close-up of Lennox's drooling chops.

'Grrrrruffff!' the white bulldog snarled.

'Watch you don't blind 'im!' Bernie squawked. 'What're you doin' with that bloomin' thing, any'ow?'

'Nothing!' Tom said, nipping off double quick.

He searched in the hedge bordering the main road. Sniff-sniff! Yuck! Hmm, there had definitely been a fox under here at some time, but there were no fresh footprints in the crunchy white frost.

Whee! Back on the field, the refereee blew the whistle for offside and allowed Elton a free-kick.

'C'mon, the Canaries!' their small gang of supporters trilled.

Their beefy captain took the free-kick and belted it into the back of the net.

1–0 to Elton.

Tom saw Jack Farthing try to argue with the referee, who was having none of it. 'Goal!' she insisted, then sent the ball back to the centre line.

OK, so the fox had slunk through the hedge. He'd made his way across the front lawn, down into Bernie's basement, where it would be nice and warm. He'd found a quiet corner to curl up in and pass the night–until a skateboard had whizzed through the window and ruined his peace.

What then? Had the fox stayed put for one more night? Had he still been in his lair when the first intruder broke in through the boarded-up window, and only scarpered when Tom put in his puzzled appearance? And if so, where had he chosen to hide next?

Tom pondered for a while. The Elton fans cheered their team on. Little Jimmy Black was felled by a savage tackle within a metre of the penalty area. Jack clamoured

for a penalty, but Miss R refused. When the game started again, Big Jack went in with one of his speciality high tackles and the ref blew loudly on her whistle.

'Off!' she ordered, pointing at the dressing-room.

'Not again!' Rowbridge fans moaned.

Jack argued back, waving his arms and pushing his ugly mug into the ref's face.

'Off!' She pointed and showed him the red card. So Jack walked, his temper still blazing, pushing through the Elton fans, stomping up the slope towards the school.

'What're you grinning at?' he snarled at Tom, who hadn't moved quickly enough out of his way.

Flash! The camera went off again. A second savage face appeared on the tiny, digital screen.

Jack swiped at it with the back of his hand, and Tom managed to dart away just in time. Whoops! He juggled then caught Nick's precious camera. Moments didn't

come any stickier than this!

'Did they do you for the break-in yet?' Stinky demanded, his hot breath pouring out in clouds of steam.

'No. And I told you–it wasn't me!' Tom was sick of Jack Farthing. He caught sight of Lola Kidman in amongst the spectators, her back turned to the pitch, watching Jack and him arguing. 'What is it to you? Why are you so interested?' he demanded, as Jack carried on sneering.

'You thought you were so big and tough on that weedy skateboard, didn't you, Beanie-Baby? Showin' off in front of everyone!'

That was it! Tom realised why Jack had it in for him. 'Weedy skateboard...showing off!' Yeah, Jack couldn't skate and he was jealous! Jack was the big, tough leader of the gang, yet he couldn't grind or kick-flip or shove-it!

'OK, when was the last time you ollied down a flight of stone steps?' Tom demanded now.

Jack swore at Tom, then shouldered him aside.

In the distance, Lola started the long walk up the hill towards them.

Whee! The referee blew for a Rowbridge goal. Kingsley leaped and punched the air, fell to his knees and was smothered by Jimmy and Kalid.

'Just you wait!' Jack grunted over his shoulder at Tom. 'I'm gonna find Bernie and dob you in!'

'There'll be no need for that!' a voice said from the depths of the cellars.

Tom and Jack spun round to see the King of Rowbridge Junior and his waddling sidekick emerge from their office. Bernie held up a long, shiny object, brandishing it like a sword. It glittered in the sun's rays.

The ruler! Tom gasped and tottered back. At last the caretaker had discovered the one object that would link Tom with the crime he hadn't even committed.

TOTALLY
TOM

TCB

'T. C. B!' Slowly Bernie read out the initials. 'I don't know what the "C" stands for, but I'd bet my life that "T" is for Thomas and "B" is for Bean!'

He put his broad hand on Tom's skinny shoulder to make his arrest. 'Gotcha!' he roared. 'And this time it's definitely, without a doubt, one hundred per cent certain the end of the line for you, sonny Jim!'

Seven

Tom's future looked bleak.

March-march-march! Bernie kept a firm hold and steered him towards the Head's office. The empty school echoed to the sound of their feet.

What now? Tom glanced up and down the Head's corridor. No way would Waymann be in on a Saturday morning.

'You–wait 'ere!' the caretaker ordered.

Then, 'Lennox, sit! Watch his every move, you 'ear!'

The bulldog bared his fangs and pressed Tom back against the wall, while Bernie stomped into the office and made a call.

'Mrs Waymann's on her way!' he announced two minutes later.

'Gerruff!' Lennox the Bouncer growled. *Don't move, or you're dead!*

'Oh, and by the way, I phoned your mum and dad. They'll be here by the time the Head arrives!'

Tom didn't make a sound, but inside he groaned. Oh no, not his mum and dad! He pictured the looks on their faces–the Oh-Tom-How-Could-You? expressions, the tears in his Mum's eyes. With a cold grin, Bernie waved the evidence in front of Tom's face. 'Try arguing your way out of this one,' he sneered, before stomping off for his mid-morning cuppa.

The next few minutes seemed to go on forever. Tom's mouth went dry, his palms

turned wet with sweat. Thump-thump; his heart beat against his ribs.

How bad was this? Bernie King had left him pinned against the wall by Lennox and the seconds were ticking by. There was no escape.

The bulldog squatted at Tom's feet, top lip curled, showing his teeth.

Tom gazed up at the high ceiling, down at the floor. He looked left and right, waiting for a split-second chance to leg it.

'Herrrruff!' *Don't even think about it!* the dog said.

Then there was silence.

Happy now? the voice in his head nagged. *Well done, Tom. You're about to get yourself kicked out of school!*

Tom felt his bottom lip quiver. His eyes pricked with tears.

But then he bit his lip and blinked hard. No way would they catch him crying!

'Hrrruff!' For the first time, Lennox's gaze strayed from Tom's face. He glanced down

the corridor towards Mrs Waymann's private cloakroom, sniffing noisily. Then he pricked his ears and eased himself up off his fat haunches.

He took a heavy step towards the cloakroom.

Now was Tom's chance to scarper. He would run away to America and no one would find him, ever again! He would join a gang of skateboarders in California and wear the peak of his cap backwards forever!

Huff-huff! Lennox padded down the corridor. The cloakroom door stood slightly open, and there was definitely a smell drifting out.

A bad, strong animal smell...a sharp, nose-wrinkling, dark, dog-like stink...

Tom gasped. Lennox prowled on; sniff-sniff-snuffle-grrrr!

The door opened wider, the smell grew worse.

And then out burst THE FOX! He sprang from the dark room, into the open. His sharp white teeth were bared, his bright yellow eyes glaring. Tom watched him sail through the air, teeth snapping. He saw him sink those teeth into Fat Lennox's well-padded neck.

THE FOX! Tom raised Nick's camera, aimed and took a photograph. Flash!

The corridor was flooded with sudden bright light.

The two animals were locked in battle, rolling, grappling, snapping and snarling; a mass of reddish-brown and white fur, legs and teeth.

Flash! Tom took a second picture, just to make sure.

Then there was a scream: 'Tom!'

Footsteps came running. The fox and the dog stopped fighting. Lennox backed off and the intruder fled. Sleek and silent, he sped past Beth and Harry Bean, past the Headteacher and the caretaker, out of the main entrance and into the frosty day.

'Tom, are you OK?' Beth rushed and gathered him in one of her hugs. He disappeared inside a flurry of fleece jacket and warm woollen scarf.

'Gerroff, Mum!' Tom pulled himself free. OK, so he might still be in deep trouble here, but at least he had THE picture!

'Aha!' Mrs Waymann watched the fox flash across the front lawn. She sniffed the air and identified the stink. 'So that's it. It's not bad drains at all! Now I can ring the Health and Safety people and let them know we've solved the problem. School can remain open after all!'

'Yes, and you can thank our Tom for flushing it out,' Harry cut in. 'Whatever else he might have done, he deserves credit for that.'

'No, Dad, it wasn't me!' Tom's brain worked at megabyte speed and he decided for once in his life that telling the truth was best. 'It was all down to Lennox. He found the fox and scared it off. He's the one you should thank!'

Wow, that was hard! But it worked. Tom saw Bernie King's stubbly head go up and his shoulders back. A proud smile lit up his broad face. 'Come 'ere, boy!' he grunted at his dog. 'You deserve a slap-up dinner for this, there's a good boy!'

Licking his lips, Lennox wagged his stumpy tail.

Hmm, now the dog would take the blame for keeping the school open. Good thinking! And Tom would be able to show the photographs to Kingsley, Bex, Ryan, Sasha, Kalid and three hundred other kids...'See, I told you there was a fox in Bernie's basement. Now d'you believe me!'

'Very well, Mr King. Why don't you take Lennox and clean him up while I deal with Thomas Bean.' Mrs Waymann took charge, sidestepping the slavering heavyweight and marching Tom and his mum and dad

into her room.

'Remember the ruler with his initials on!' the caretaker called as the door slammed shut in his face. 'I put it on your desk. Tell 'im he can't wriggle out of that one!'

'S-o-o-o!' Before Waymann settled behind her desk, she wafted lavender air spray all around her room to kill the smell of fox. 'Hisssss-hisss!' right in Tom's face.

He choked. He heard the air squeeze out of her cushion as she sank into her chair. Behind him, his mum and dad stood silent and worried.

'So, Mr and Mrs Bean, I'm afraid we have a serious situation on our hands.' Waymann leaned her elbows on the desk and made a roof shape with her fingertips. 'Mr King is accusing Thomas of breaking into his office in order to get his skateboard back, and I must say the evidence of the ruler is pretty convincing.'

'Oh, Tom!' Beth sighed.

He could feel the how-could-you stare burn into the skin on his back.

'What do you have to say for yourself?' Mrs Waymann demanded.

Tom sighed and didn't answer. He knew they would never believe him.

'Come on, tell me the truth, Tom!' The Head picked up Tom's metal ruler and tapped it on the desk. 'How else did this

get into the basement if you didn't break in and drop it there?

Tap-tap. Tom closed his eyes and tried to think of an excuse. Please miss, that's not my ruler! Please Miss, someone must've planted it there! Nope, they were useless. The ruler was staring him in the face.

So he did it; he told the truth!

'Please miss, I didn't break in. Maybe I would've done, but I didn't need to. The door was already open!'

'Oh, Tom!' Beth's sigh filled the room.

Mrs Waymann arched her thin eyebrows. A likely story! 'Is this what you intend to tell the police when they arrive?'

Tom felt faint, his knees shook. Even now, the cop cars were blaring their way towards school, for real this time!

'It's true!' he insisted. 'It wasn't me!'

A knock at the door made Waymann frown. 'Go away!' she cried. 'I'm busy!'

But the door opened and Lola Kidman stepped in wearing her blue and white

supporters' hat and long striped scarf. She was out of breath, her brown eyes were shining, and long wisps of dark, wavy hair were escaping from under the hat.

'I can't see you now. Come back on Monday.' Waymann had risen from her flowery cushion and was crossly waving Lola away.

'Please, Mrs Waymann, Mr Wright sent me. He wants you to have a little word with Jack Farthing.'

'Later, after I've dealt with Tom Bean!'

But Lola refused to be shooed out. 'This is *to do* with Tom, Miss.'

And before Waymann could ask any questions, the PE teacher had marched Jack into the room. 'Tell them, Lola!' Mr Wright insisted. 'Take it easy, explain it to them one step at a time!'

'And did you, Lola? Did you really see Jack breaking into Bernie King's basement?'

Rowbridge Juniors had drawn their match

2–2. 'We were robbed!' Jimmy complained. But now Kalid, Ryan, Kingsley and the rest could catch up with the Jack Farthing story.

'The Head kicked him out!'

'He's never coming back, not even for his books!'

'He confessed everything!'

'He set Tom up, the snake! Tom nearly got kicked out instead!'

Word flew around the changing room and spilled out into the playground, where everyone crowded round Lola and Tom.

'You saw him do it, Lola!' Jimmy cried. 'You caught him red handed. Wow, how lucky is that!'

Lola grinned then shrugged. 'That's what I made Jack believe.'

'But you didn't really?' prissy Bex demanded.

'What's the difference? I got him to own up, didn't I?'

Yeah, Tom thought. *Yes, yes, yes!* There in the Head's office, Jack had confessed.

One step at a time, Lola had put Mrs Waymann in the picture.

'I saw Jack being sent off by the ref and I followed him,' she'd explained. 'I had it out with him, said it was time to face facts: he was the one who'd broken into Bern–er–Mr King's office to steal Tom's skateboard. Only he was interrupted by a fox, and the fox attacked him and scratched his arm and sent him running like a scaredy-cat...'

Yes, the scratch! The bandaged arm. How come Tom had never made the link? But he recalled how Mr Wright had made Jack show the headteacher his bandaged arm. The white gauze had been unwound slowly to show the long, red marks made by a sharp-clawed creature...

'...Well, Jack couldn't deny it, could he?' Lola had pointed out. 'He did have a major strop out in the playground, though. He got me in this armlock and I had to kick his shin to get away. By this time, Mr Wright had seen us fighting and he ran up from

the football pitch. Then I told him what had happened, and that's how come we're here now!'

'Phew! What did Waymann do?' Kalid asked softly in the wondering silence.

'She kicked Jack out,' Lola told them, grinning at Tom. 'And aren't we all sad about it–NOT!'

'Like this!' Tom leaned on the kicktail and raised the nose of his brand new board. He whizzed past a crowd of kids in the skate park, pulling a wheelie at 20 miles per hour.

The board was an early Chrimbo present from the whole Bean clan. His mum, dad and three big brothers had clubbed together and bought him the best pro deck in the shop. They said he deserved it for what Jack Farthing had done to him.

'Like this?' Lola tried the move on Tom's beaten up old board. It was her first time, so she was a bit wobbly.

'Try it!' Tom had insisted. 'Don't lean too hard on the tail, otherwise the deck hits the ground.'

Lola learned fast. Soon she was up to speed with wheelies, kickturns and slides. 'I like this board,' she grinned.

'You should've seen Bernie's face when he was forced to give it back.' Tom gloated over the memory.

'As long as you never bring it back into school!' Waymann had made him promise. 'And don't knock people down in the street!'

So they were in the park, and Tom was teaching Lola radical moves. He yelled instructions and caught her when she bailed.

'Whoo-ooo, Tom Bean fancies Lola Kidman!' Danielle trilled. 'Witty-woo-woo!'

Tom rose above the insult. 'Take no notice,' he advised.

It was getting dark and beginning to spit with rain. He had one more trick to teach

Lola before they went home. But first, he was still dying to solve a mystery. 'How did you know the fox had scratched Jack's arm?' he wondered, as they stood in line waiting their turn. 'Had you seen under the bandage?'

Lola shook her head, then jammed her cap down more firmly.

'Then how?' Tom insisted.

'I just knew. It's a girl-thing.'

'You guessed!'

She nodded happily. 'You could say that. I was right though, wasn't I?'

'Tom Bean fancies Lola!' the girls cried out as the pair set off to tic-tac down the park.

'Kickturn left, right, left...!' Tom yelled.

She turned right, left, right–smack into Tom!

They landed in a tangled heap while their boards went hurtling on.

'Live to surf, dudes!' Kingsley commented as he acid-dropped out of the vert then smoothly ollied over them.

'Yeah!' Tom sighed. Another bruise, a first dent in his new board. So what? He turned up his face to feel the damp, cold drizzle. Tomorrow was another kickturning, fakie tricking, sliding grinding, flying through the air type of day!

Look out for more
Totally Tom adventures!

Watch Out, Wayne

Jenny Oldfield

Life's tough for Tom. He offers to be best mates with new boy, Wayne, but it only lands him in trouble–again! OK, maybe giving Wayne a CRASH course in skateboarding wasn't so smart.
But Tom meant well. Honest!

Get Lost, Lola

Jenny Oldfield

Tom is TOTALLY disgusted. Lola–aka, Little Miss Superglue–says she fancies him. Ergh! And Lola knows a shameful secret about Tom. If he doesn't agree to be her boyfriend, then the whole school will know it, too...Uh-oh! But would Lola really be that devious and mean?

Keep the Noise Down, Kingsley

Jenny Oldfield

Tom has a rival at school. Kingsley is a mega annoying show off! He's lary, he's brash, and he's really getting on everyone's nerves! Tom needs to find a way to break it to Kingsley that he's got to pipe down! But how?

Drop Dead, Danielle

Jenny Oldfield

Mean and mardy 'dob-them-in' Danielle is on Tom's case again-accusing him of flooding the school cloakroom! *As if.* Danielle says she's going to tell on Tom–and she probably will! Tom needs to prove it wasn't him–but how?

Don't Make Me Laugh, Liam

Jenny Oldfield

Tom's cousin Liam is coming over from Dublin. Wicked! Liam is just like Tom–only ten times noisier, and even more of a joker–he'll probably give him a few handy tips! Uh-oh. As if Tom really needs any encouragement...